The LEGEND —of the— FOURTH KING

The

LEGEND

—— *of the* ——

FOURTH
KING

EDZARD SCHAPER

Illustrations by Tanja Butler
Translated by Peter Heinegg

A Crossroad Book
The Crossroad Publishing Company
New York

The Crossroad Publishing Company
370 Lexington Avenue, New York, NY 10017

First published in 1961 as *Die Legende vom vierten König* by Jakob Hegner Verlag, Cologne. Republished by Artemis Verlag, Zurich and Munich, copyright © 1975.

English translation copyright © 1999 by The Crossroad Publishing Company.

Printed in the United States of America

Library of Congress Cataloging-in-Publication Data

Schaper, Edzard, 1908–
    [Legende vom vierten König. English]
    The legend of the fourth king / by Edzard Schaper ; translated by
Peter Heinegg.
        p.   cm.
    ISBN 0-8245-1814-4
    1. Magi Legends Fiction.   I. Heinegg, Peter.   II. Title.
PT2638.A68L313   1999
833'.912 – dc21   99-31366

1   2   3   4   5   6   7   8   9   10   04   03   02   01   00   99

WHEN THE CHRIST CHILD was about to be born in Bethlehem, the star announcing his birth appeared not only to the wise kings in the East but also to a king in far Russia. He was no great and mighty lord; he wasn't especially rich or remarkably clever, or a devotee of magical arts. He was a king with an open mind and a good, kindly heart; he loved people and was very good-natured, companionable, and by no means averse to a joke. They called him "the little czar." The little czar had learned from his fathers, and the fathers of his fathers, that one day a star would appear in the skies and announce the coming of the supreme ruler of the whole world. He knew that the one ruling over Russia at that time was to set out to pay homage to this greater king. This prophecy had been treasured and passed on from generation to generation.

The little czar burst with joy when he realized that the star heralding the grandest event the earth had ever seen had appeared in the skies while he, still a young man, was ruling the country. He decided to set off at once. He didn't take a large entourage with him, not even his most faithful servant. That wasn't his style, and, besides, nothing was known of the whereabouts of this birth of the greatest ruler, or how long the journey might be. The little czar wished to undertake this quest alone.

He asked that his favorite pony, Vanyka, be saddled — no proud steed for warfare this was, just one of those little tough and unbeatable Russian ponies. Vanyka had a shaggy mane with such a heavy forelock that his eyes could hardly make out the path in front of him. But he was tireless and undemanding, just as one needs on a long journey.

"But wait!" thought the little czar. "One does not go empty-handed to offer homage to a royal personage, especially to the highest of all kings." The little czar pondered for a long time what to take with him — something that represented the riches of his land and the hard work of its people. It needed to fit into his saddlebags and, even more, had to honor the newborn lord.

"Wise people," the Russian ruler thought, "tend to judge the kingdoms of this world by the handicrafts of their women." So he took several rolls of the finest, most beautiful linen woven from Russian flax. Along with that he packed some of the most noble furs that his hunters had bagged in the wintry woods and tanned until they were as soft as velvet or chamois. "Seeing these," the little czar thought, "everyone, not to mention this all-wise baby, will see that even in winter my people don't lie around doing nothing — although sitting by one of our great warm stoves, with kvass and lightly salted cucumbers is, indeed, heavenly."

From the river valleys where his workers panned for gold, he ordered numerous little leather pouches filled with the magic dust that creates all the ups and downs in this world. From the mountains where the ablest miners dug deep in the most hidden mineshafts, known to none of his other subjects and never spoken of, he quickly increased the supply of rare and precious stones in his treasury. The most beautiful and valuable ones he took with him as a gift from his kingdom.

And finally, heeding woman's wit — and, indeed, he had heard that that was the only thing able to keep the world from flying off its hinges when the wisdom of kings ran out — he let his mother add a small clay jar of honey, for nectar gathered by fat, velvety bees in linden trees. Children of all kinds need this honey, his mother said. And if this child

had come from heaven, as the old prophecy said, the honey of a Russian linden would surely remind him of his better home.

These were the gifts that the little czar took along with him. He carefully entrusted all his business to his people, telling them how they should handle things until his return. Then he rode off on Vanyka one night when the star was shining most brightly. He rode all the way through his kingdom, but the star wouldn't stand still. Now he had to cross the borders into an unknown world. He did so, but foreign countries, of course, were different and more difficult than the familiar earth of one's home. Day after day he traveled, sometimes even after dark. At times he thought the star's long tail almost touched the earth, and for a moment he wanted to grasp it and let it pull him right up to the land of glory.

But that didn't happen. The only thing pulling him was his own desire to honor the greatest ruler of all times and places; and he strove never to let this desire slacken or wane, no matter how absorbing or confusing the alien world around him might be.

He saw so much that he had not known before. The good things he observed carefully so that he might introduce them to Russia. The bad things grieved and troubled him more than when he was in Russia, where he had the means and power to command change. His compassion awakened as he saw the just languish and the righteous in misery. He helped where he could, with words and deeds. And when on the road again and all by himself, he thought all the more passionately about how much the world needed a new and universal ruler. The persecuted needed protection, the oppressed longed to be lifted up, prisoners had to be set free, the sick asked for healing, and the just demanded reward. For all of these people the new ruler would care; so promised the old prophecy the little czar followed.

H E HAD ALREADY JOURNEYED for two or three moons when one night the star sailed across the sky in particular splendor. Vanyka trotted vigorously after it while the little czar rode lost in dreams of his faraway homeland. But all of a sudden a rather strange encounter took place. At first he made out what seemed to be hills moving in the darkness. When he drew closer, an elegant entourage appeared, likely preferring the cool of the night for their journey. Or were they following the star as he was? Only these lords and their retinue rode not horses but camels, which shuffled past as if shod with felt. What had looked like moving hills were the humps of these heavily laden beasts.

When the lively trot of the Russian pony caught up with the party, the accompanying servants immediately clustered around their three lords, fencing them in as if guarding against robbers. But any misunderstanding soon vanished. The little czar, affable as he was, greeted the unexpected company. He asked the three lords where they came from and where they were headed. They named kingdoms in the East from which they had set out and of which the little Russian king had never heard anyone speak. Their destination, it turned out, was his own: the place over which the star would stand still. There, they said, it had been revealed to them that a child would be born who was to be the greatest king, the most learned wise man and physician, the highest priest of all times and places. They must pay homage to this child, they said, and adore him.

The little czar was beside himself with astonishment. He told them that he had set off from Russia for the very same reason. The three lords from the East had heard of Russia, but they seemed to think it was a very dark, wild, and freezing cold land where it simply wasn't worthwhile being king. All through the night and until the morning the little czar sought to win them over, to convince them that, indeed, Russia was the best and dearest country in the world. But he didn't quite succeed.

When morning finally dawned and he could see with whom he had been speaking so freely all night, he felt rather abashed. Compared with all their splendor and dignity swaying on the backs of these camels, he seemed a mere rascal. Looking at the many busy attendants, he wondered for a moment whether it might not have been smarter to bring along a few of his own most faithful servants to wait on him. Even so, his very best people could not have matched these lackeys and all the courtly polish they had copied from their three masters.

The little czar looked down in embarrassment at his dusty, threadbare riding coat. With their measured silence the three mighty lords from the East seemed to be saying that in the light of day he looked far too small to have made such a commotion at night. Those three were altogether the strangest people the little czar had ever laid eyes on; yet during the last few months he had seen some very strange things indeed. One of the kings, with a long, waxed, painted beard, was about as white as the people he knew, the second was yellow like a linden tree blossom, and the third a rich, beautiful black.

The star pointing the way had now set. They were approaching a village, where the lords wanted to look for an inn. The little czar was used to sleeping behind a barn with his saddle for a pillow. Out on the fields, morning dew still sparkled, with the sun rising as if to set fire to the earth. The three kings praised the spectacle, but the little czar got completely carried away. Though feeling dusty and insignificant, he wanted to make his mark in the company of such exotic splendor. "But a few pearls from my precious Russia," he sang, "sparkle so much more beautifully than even the morning dew!" He reached into his saddlebag, pulled out a little leather pouch, and strewed its contents — the pearls for the divine child — in a wide arc across the gleaming field. It was as if they were seedlings of his vanity and of his love for the precious land of his mothers and fathers.

The three lords fell silent, stunned by this exuberance. It was quite a while before the one with the long beard asked him: "Were those pearls?"

"Surely," said the little czar. "Actually..." Only now did it occur to him that they had been meant for the greater king, but he was too ashamed to admit that, so he didn't finish the sentence. Then

he added abruptly: "Russia has so many more of the same."

"Pearls are tears," said the stranger with the long beard. "Why do you sow your tears in alien soil, my brother lord?"

"Ah, that is just what I set out for," said the little czar with jaunty carelessness. "I still have my laughter!" But he wasn't feeling as jolly as he pretended. With every mile they rode together, he increasingly felt that the three lords didn't believe that he was searching for the same destination they were. To make matters worse, they seemed to think that he was not at all worthy to be a vassal of this supreme ruler. In the remaining time he spent with them, the three held such learned conversations with one another that he couldn't follow them at all. He would have preferred conversing with one of their servants, except that he couldn't understand them either.

When they arrived at the inn, everything had

been prepared to receive them, since the three kings had sent a herald to announce their coming. So they went to enjoy a proper rest even though it was broad daylight. The little czar, too lowly to accompany the three lords, and — for the honor of Russia and himself — too proud to stay with their servants, refused to play the awkward role of an extra. As was his custom, he tied the feed bag on his pony, took off the saddlebags and the saddle, and lay down his head to sleep in the barn all by himself.

H E SLEPT SPLENDIDLY and dreamed of kvass and lightly salted cucumbers, as if he were lying by the warm stove back home in Russia. Toward evening he awoke to a groan that resonated with all the world's grief. He rubbed his eyes in astonishment, for he had thought he was alone. Obviously, though, someone had slipped into the barn after him. It was a poor young woman who had crept in hoping to find shelter, for she was about to give birth. And while the little czar had slept in comfort, her baby girl had been born. No one else was there to help the young mother and child. Alas, this was a task he had no knowledge of, yet his heart wouldn't take no for an answer. The little czar brought some food and drink from the inn, and as the young mother had absolutely nothing in her purse he gave her a few pinches of gold from his little leather pouches.

But the baby still looked miserable. With a serious wrinkle on his brow, the little czar kept looking at her wretched nakedness. "Oh, you poor little bird!" he said. "What a wastrel your father must be to give you nothing more than your thin skin to begin life in this world." With that he went off, grabbed one of his saddlebags, pulled out a roll of delicate linen, and cut a half dozen of the finest full Russian-measure diapers.

When he had seen to all the necessities and mother and child could securely await the coming night, the little czar saddled his pony and bade farewell to the woman. "In my country," he said, "you would be better off." And he went on about his beloved Russia, where the poor could count on

compassion, though he did not tell her about the royal position he held there.

"In my country," the poor woman said with a frail voice, "you should be the king. But I don't count for anything at all. I can only make you the king of my heart. That I will surely do from this moment on."

"See," the little czar said happily to himself. "I have, of course, given away some of the gold and linen meant for the greatest king. But in exchange I now have my own country even overseas, and perhaps heart-land isn't so bad. If only the king of all times and places would understand..."

When he led his pony into the courtyard of the inn, the place lay wide open and empty. The caravan of the three mighty foreign rulers had set off at the first ray from the star. People in the village were now talking about the star with the long tail, which, they were certain, pointed out something highly unusual.

The little czar shook his head soberly. For the first time on his journey fear crept into his heart, and he had a dim sense that he might have failed or missed something. But then he pulled himself together, entrusted the poor woman and her child to the village people, and rode away.

He rode and rode. He rode that night and the next and all the following nights that month. He had long since sung all the songs from his homeland that he could remember to bolster his and Vanyka's courage at night. He had completely lost track of the caravan and the three kings from the East. It seemed that the road had swallowed them up. When he asked about them, people gave him cryptic answers, as if someone had told them to pass on false information. That was strange, for the country was at peace just then, and the gates of all the towns and hamlets stood open even at night.

Still, as long as the great star hung in the sky

and he was free to choose his path, there wasn't too much concern — caravan or no caravan. Of course, he would have preferred to be with the three kings when paying his respects to the royal baby, not so much because he wanted their glamour to spill over onto him but because company tends to give a little bravery to the shy.

Yet the people he traveled with by day never got the impression that he was especially shy. There was after all a king within him, accustomed to command and also to judge. The farther he rode, the more unjustly he thought the countries were governed and the harder the lot of their people. Disease spread everywhere, and woe to those doomed to sickness, for their dying would drag on for years with no one to nurse or care for them. The whip prevailed where the just scepter should have, and human beings were turning into commodities. The little czar was appalled. Only now could he measure how longingly the king of kings had been awaited, generation after generation. For all these people he was to be born.

While the little czar had absolutely no wish to supplant this new ruler — he certainly didn't understand how to rule as well as the new ruler would, even though he was only a child — he gave help where the need was overwhelming in anticipation of the king to come. And when offered thanks he said that thanks were really merited by the other, the greater king to come. Thus his supply of gold began to shrink, and soon he could count the days before he would have to trade in his precious stones for money.

In fact, this day came even sooner than he had expected. One evening he saw two enormous plantation foremen battering their emaciated serfs with canes, shouting that the men and women had not worked enough. Many collapsed like corpses beneath the hail of blows. Without hesitation the little czar bought their freedom.

In addition to requiring a great deal of money, this affair took a lot of time, and he wasn't finished at star rise. For the first time on his whole journey the little czar spent the night in one place. He sat amid the freed serfs, who cheered him as their redeemer, and he watched the star wander across the sky. His star that was...but he didn't follow it. Vanyka, used to trotting at this time of night, tossed his head in surprise.

The next day the little czar rode off for the first time in bright sunshine, although he had nothing to show him the way except his own intuition. But he wanted to put behind him quickly the place where they had celebrated him like a savior. A wave of afterthoughts furrowed his brow as he rode along on Vanyka. The pony squinted in the unfamiliar sunlight, and the little czar wondered whether the good was always the right as well.

The people whose freedom he had bought had come to him early that morning, asking who was going to feed them now. They were used to having their overseers and torturers brandish not just the cane but the soup ladle too. On this, the first idle morning of their lives, they had tasted neither the one nor the other. Now they were hungry; they wanted to eat. Before he rode away, the little czar had given them some more gold so they could buy food for three days. And then he had told them they were to go out and work like free men and women. But scarcely had he left the place than he began to doubt whether that would happen. Perhaps their ways were set and change was not possible.

That day, in bright sunshine, the little czar counted the leather pouches he had left and shuddered. There were fewer than he had thought, far fewer. "Perhaps," he thought, by way of excusing himself, "some thieves robbed me during the day without my noticing it. I sleep so soundly, and when I dream of kvass and lightly salted cucumbers, anyone could simply carry me away. Not to mention the fact that someone could open the saddlebags..." But deep down he didn't really believe it; these were just the dodges of a guilty conscience.

He decided to be very spartan and to stop dipping into the treasure of the supreme ruler. He wouldn't want the great king to think poorly of his beloved homeland. Besides, he comforted himself a bit too eagerly, there were still a few rolls of fine linen and the furs. Also, the little honey jar would offset many, many other things, because the honey had been gathered from linden trees by the round, golden-skinned bees of Russia. But, even before the evening fell, the little czar had once again broken his resolutions. He despaired of himself. Two lepers along the way had awakened his compassion, and he had sliced a whole roll of fine linen into bandages to cover their open sores in the hope that their suffering could be alleviated and the swarms of loathsome flies would leave them alone.

"Now I'm entering the mountains," the little czar thought. "The air will get purer, and I won't see any more flies on the pus-filled wounds of lepers, so I won't be tempted to give more things away." But the more he tried to shake off temptation and weakness, the harder it became for him. "Actually," he thought to himself, "these aren't weaknesses at all. Can I help it if God sends quite different necessities my way than he sends other people? I'd be surprised if the greatest of all kings had no understanding of this. Gifts in homage are all very well, but giving help to his future subjects when they need it is even better. Besides, when I tell him all the things I really wanted to bring along with me, how could he not believe?" And so from one mile to the next he wove for himself an ever finer web of excuses for why he had to do what he did and why he would have to go on doing the same.

As he set off into the mountains, the evening came on dark and cloudy, for winter was near. Only one time did he see his star, but then it was hidden by rain. "Jump, Vanyka, jump! Bite it in the tail!" the little czar cried out boldly and urged his pony on, but that whole night he rode without knowing where he was going. When morning came, he could only be glad that he and Vanyka were still in one piece, so trackless and desolate was the region. And when the sun rose, he found a merchant who had been attacked by robbers. The evening before they had struck him down, leaving him nothing but his shirt.

"Oh, my friend," said the little czar, full of pity, "you look like a cherub who's flown off course, naked as you are. You'll have to be helped for compassion's sake." First he bound up the victim's wounds, though the fine linen seemed to be shouting in his ears when he tore bandages from the roll. He chided it in his heart: stanching blood is as noble as wrapping a baby's behind. Then he refreshed the wounded man with food and drink.

The little czar looked at the naked man, looked at his pony, and scratched behind his ear. "Vanyka has a beautiful long tail and a thick, furry mane. But even if I cut it all off, I couldn't weave it into a suit of clothes for you.... It won't do any good. I'll have to part with a few pelts and another roll of linen or you'll freeze at nightfall."

So the assaulted merchant ended up wearing sable and the finest wedding linen when he returned to his people. The little czar continued to follow his star, Vanyka's saddlebags practically empty. By now the bags seemed to be full of holes, so quickly did even his last supplies dwindle away.

WHEN THE LITTLE CZAR had been on the road for a year, he could feel the bottom of all his saddlebags. The linen had gone to the naked and sick, the furs to people shivering with cold, the gold and precious stones — except the pearls he had spilled in his early outburst of high spirits — to the needy and enslaved. The only thing left was his mother's gift, the small clay jar. The little czar carefully raised the lid covering the honey and let the sun mirror itself in the liquid.

He sat by the side of the road, letting Vanyka graze. In recent days he had hardly tasted oats. He was shaggier than and alarmingly thin. He had gotten a pony-year older, which equals more than a human year. The little czar gazed in ecstasy at the shining mirror of the yellow nectar and saw in his mind's eye the green-golden fire of the blossoming linden trees back in Russia. There they stood, bathing in the sun, every one of them a cloud of fragrance and buzzing with bees.

The little czar was overcome by a boundless longing for home. "Ah," he thought, "better to be a short-lived bee at home than an unknown king in a foreign land. And better to fly off to the lindens than to run after the stars." He had been a whole year on his journey by now, and no end was in sight. Life abroad had become miserable. What at first had seemed new and exciting had become dull, and now that he had given away everything, he talked with no one but Vanyka. He had become lonelier than he could have ever imagined.

The first wild bee, burning with hunger after the

winter and lured by the perfume of Russian linden trees, alighted on the rim of the tiny clay jar
and began sucking the honey. The little czar didn't
see her, or she flew away too quickly for him to
make anything of it. Only when three and four and
then thirty, forty, and more bees came humming
along did he notice that they meant to rob him of
his last treasure. "Get away! Away!" he shouted as
he swatted at them while groping for the jar's lid.
He had laid it aside but now couldn't find it —
without realizing it he had been sitting right on
it. Now the shining lid of his jar was covered with
bees, all licking the sweet honey from home. When
the little czar reached out and jumped up with the
jar in his hand, he found himself in a cloud of glit-
tering wings, and the more he shook the jar, trying
to fight off the lustful bees, the more ferociously
they stung him.

"Get away! Away!" the little czar shouted over
and over, but this time the words were meant for

himself. He wanted to flee on Vanyka's back and carry the jar to safety. But Vanyka...Vanyka himself was set upon by the bees. He galloped in circles, kicked wildly, and twisted his head to one side and then to the other. Head-down, Vanyka plunged into the wind across the fields and then rolled over on the ground to crush the winged pests entangled in his mane.

The little czar could hardly see Vanyka because his eyes were swollen shut from all the bee stings. He still held the jar with his right hand, which by now was a swarming mass of bees, and felt like he had dipped it into a stream of fire. "Yes, yes," he thought, more in sorrow than in rage, "go on, gobble me up alive." He would have liked to cry, but his eyelids were all sealed up now, so that he could not even weep. All he was able to do was surrender: to the burning pain, the sadness, and the darkness in which his whole world, including the sun, seemed to drown.

And so he remained sitting there, hoping that no one would find him in such misery and that the pony would return once the bees quit their attack. Vanyka now was his only treasure. The little czar's heart was filled with discontent — about the prophecy that had made him travel; about the star that wouldn't stand still; about the greatest king of all times and places, who had summoned him from afar; about these alien lands that had so deceived and misled him; about the three kings, who he felt had betrayed him; and about the ingratitude of the ones he had helped. Only with himself did he not quarrel.

When finally he could again open his eyes, there was no way to know what day it was. It had long been dark around him, and in his feverish pain the little czar hadn't been able to count days and nights. The world still seemed the same. Vanyka was grazing nearby, the saddle hanging lopsided from his deeply creased back. The saddlebags lolled limp as bellows.

The little czar rolled his head, gazed out of his still swollen eyes, and saw that the honey jar in his red, misshapen right hand was empty — completely cleaned out. And no bee could be heard buzzing. In a fit of black despair he hurled his mother's jar in a high arc. It shattered against a rock. He staggered to Vanyka and kicked the pony's croup. Then he swung into the saddle and rode off from this place of disaster, his eyes filled with tears. He cursed all the creatures that had robbed him, and he condemned creation itself.

A few days later he was kneeling alongside Vanyka. In his own despair the little czar had treated the pony unjustly. Now, stretched out on all fours, Vanyka lay on the ground, refusing to get up. "Who will take me to my star?" the little czar asked, looking into the pony's dimming eyes. "Who will take me to my star, and who will take me back to Russia, if not you, my friend? Forgive the kick the other day. I couldn't kick myself, but, believe me, that's how I meant it!" Vanyka's nostrils quivered slightly, as if he were sniffing the fragrance of the hay of pastures back home. His head stiffened. His legs stretched out still further so that the fetlocks cracked. He almost looked like a proper horse. "I know you can't answer," said the little czar, "but you don't need to laugh so contemptuously now when I ask you." For he thought that Vanyka had bared his teeth in laughter. But the pony was already dead.

WHEN IT FINALLY DAWNED on the little czar that Vanyka was gone, he sat for many hours beside his four-legged friend, toying with the shaggy clusters of his mane. The neck he was petting grew stiffer and stiffer. At one point he brushed aside the thick curtain of the pony's forelock and tried to look him in the eye. But he couldn't endure the strange, glassy darkness there. He could think only of the waggish chuzpah, the curiosity, and the faithful patience that once dwelt in those eyes. He let the hair fall back and stood up.

For hours he worked, busily heaping up stones

from far and wide. He piled them on top of his dead friend so that the wild beasts wouldn't disturb his slumber. The first layer of stones he laid against Vanyka's cold flank and apologized again and again, for they were heavy. Then he sat down beside the stone mound and awaited the star.

The star did not appear in the first hour of the night, nor in the second, or third, or fourth. The little czar stared as hard as he could into the sky, and he cursed the wind that brought tears to his eyes. Not until long after midnight did he jump up and hasten off into the darkness. But as fast as he rushed, he couldn't move as quickly as Vanyka had, and he realized that his journey was going to last even longer now. But that wasn't all of his sorrow: night after night the pattern was repeated — the star came out late, just before morning. He didn't want to admit it, but the hours when he could see the star, far beyond the horizon toward the south, became fewer and fewer. Its tail no longer stretched into the skies but pointed down to the earth in a southerly direction.

The little czar ran aimlessly through the night. Far and wide dogs barked with suspicion, and watchmen peered out at him. "What good has come of it all?" he thought bitterly. "Feeding the hungry, clothing the naked, freeing prisoners — I have wasted all I had, only to sow the seeds of my own unhappiness ... to become king over the heart of a single poor woman. Ridiculous! I felt rather proud of it at the time. What a fool! Now, despite everything, I will arrive too late, and even if I could get there in time, I'd come as a beggar and not be allowed in."

At some point not much later came the longest night the little czar had ever known, the night when the star did not appear at all, though the sky was crisp, clear, and cloudless. From dusk until dawn he remained seated in one spot. Then he stayed there all day. Again the next night, the little czar stared motionless at the sky. The next

morning, following more his own intuition than heavenly guidance, he crept into a stable. And while falling asleep he thanked God for the kindness of this simple bed of straw, still warm from the bodies of the animals that had spent the night there.

After this second night that the star did not shine, one could actually say that the little czar had become a hobo. He walked and walked, day and night. Sometimes he walked with hope in his heart, and sometimes his heart was filled with defiance, desperation, and sorrow. He did not really have a destination anymore, or perhaps both his eyes and his soul had just lost sight of it. And the less he knew where he was going, the more he became entangled in the unhappiness and the ways of the world, a world so wicked that even the greatest of kings would never be able to cure it. And as the little czar surrendered to the darkness of his soul, it became only a matter of time until reality would follow.

45

ONE MORNING he found himself at the edge of the sea in a beautiful city. Since early morning the little czar had been sitting by the water, watching the sunrise break like mother-of-pearl in the surf. "Ah!" if only he still had some pearls to throw into the water in celebration of this wonderful sight. But suddenly he became witness to quite a wild scene. A galley making ready to sail was one man short. The missing oarsman was dead. He had been a delinquent debtor of the ship's owner, who had him condemned to serve aboard one of his galleys until the debt was paid off by the strength of his arms.

But those arms hadn't been strong enough, and the man himself had not been fit to serve on a galley. Before the vessel reached port they had thrown his corpse into the water.

Now the owner and his servants were leading the dead man's half-grown son to the ship. The debt had yet to be paid off. Alongside the boy walked his mother, still a young woman, begging the captain for mercy. He barked that he wanted nothing to do with them, but that the son had to pay off the rest of the debt and he would be put in his father's chains.

The little czar stood to one side, listening to all that was going on, including the anger and grief in his heart. He ached for the young widow, whose beauty he did not fail to notice. Her pain touched him. The boy would without doubt follow his father to an early grave in the sea. Like a lamb led to the slaughter, he stood inert and helpless, looking now at his mother, now at his tormentors. She in turn pleaded with the ship's owner; if he took her son she would have no means of support.

"First work off what you have already eaten!" he shouted with a wicked laugh. "Or do you want to come along with us? That would be some fun!"

The little czar watched the young woman. Momentarily he thought of all the girls back home whom he had looked at with pleasure but never wooed. He imagined a good life alongside a woman as gentle and faithful as this one surely was.... Suddenly the captain ordered the lad to be taken onboard. The winds were blowing favorably just then, and he was in a hurry to put the young man in irons and leave. The little czar sprang forward into the group.

"I'm going in place of the boy," he said firmly, looking the captain straight in the eye.

The next thing he heard was a mocking laugh. Then the captain sized him up, as a butcher looks over a head of cattle he's been offered to slaughter.

"Oho," he said, "he thinks he's up to it? He should think it over awhile. This will be one of many long trips if he is to pay the full debt. And for men with mutinous looks there may be a surcharge to pay...." But the captain let it be understood that the replacement was all right with him. In fact, it had taken him only a second to see that this stranger would make a stronger rower than the half-grown boy.

The little czar looked to the young widow, whose eyes were wide with bewilderment and hope. The tears and a new, timid faith on her face made her even more beautiful. His heart went out, longing to love her for the rest of his days, but how could he even think of it when all his confidence and esteem for his own life had been lost long ago?

"I will go," he said softly, and then he turned away and descended into the belly of the ship, where the foreman firmly locked the shackles around his ankles.

With this began a time in the life of the little czar that can quickly be told. And yet that time was so long, so cruelly long to live through. Almost thirty years, thirty years in the galleys! He had been naïve to let himself be put in a dead man's chains; he had not even asked the exact amount of the debt or how long he would have to row to pay it off. And ever since the irons had locked him in the answer had been: "Not for a long time yet!"

Year after year he slaved away, side by side with the world's most desperate wretches, who had wound up on the ship through their own foolishness or the cunning of others. Twice in those thirty years he managed to run away, but his legs, held so long in irons, failed to carry him fast enough. He was caught both times, and the debt he had taken over increased, though by now it had become very clear that the debt was just a pretense. Countless times when he saw his companions being so badly mistreated, he stirred up rebellion. Each time, as

the captain had announced when they were still in the harbor, a "surcharge" was added to his liability. The ship's owner he had first served under died. His son inherited the little czar as a hardworking but mutinous rower. Also, the foremen changed several times, and soon nobody remembered that he had once been chained to the bench for someone else and that all he needed to do was work off the rest of a dead man's debt.

For the little czar, this may well have been the worst and the most painful of all: gradually he and his sacrifice slipped into oblivion. Finally, he belonged to the ship as if he were just a mute part of the rigging. His history erased, he ceased to be human and became a shadow of himself. He would stare with the deeply sunken eyes of his gaunt face, yet no one could say whether he was seeing anything at all, indeed whether he was still alive. With every year his look became more like the one he had seen long ago in the eyes of Vanyka, the pony,

an expression that back then he hadn't been able
to bear.

And yet, while others couldn't have noticed, the
little czar did see, and he lived. Something was
there that kept him going, and it was all he had
left. The star that had led him to leave home in
the first place appeared constantly now. For the
ship's belly was dark enough for him to make it
out even during the day. It was like a reflection of
light falling into a deep well and splitting with its
splendor the endless darkness that surrounded the
feverish heat of the rowers' benches belowdecks.
The little czar recalled the many paths he had rid-
den, and especially he remembered the morning
when a king from the East had asked why he was
sowing his tears in alien soil.

"I still have my laughter," he had foolishly replied then. By now he had long since lost it, along
with the pearls, gold, precious stones, furs, and
linen. And as for the kingdom in her heart the poor

woman in the stable had promised him, he neither believed in it nor hoped for it anymore.

Unspeakable remorse filled his years. He had wasted everything, pointlessly thrown it all away. He was a complete failure, not to mention the fact that he would never become a vassal of the supreme ruler. By now he wasn't even worthy of the crown in his homeland. Surely someone else had long since claimed his throne, and surely he was now forgotten. But as the years passed by, he wondered more and more often why the rule of the greatest king, whom he had gone forth to pay homage to, had not shown itself by a turn for the better in the wretched life onboard the galley.

The little czar also thought of the beautiful widow for whom he had volunteered as a galley slave. He had long ago realized that he hadn't done it to ease the lot of the boy but to give the woman, the mother, a sign of his powerfully wakened love. And he found that the light of the star could shine on her face as well. He had nothing to hide or regret. But where was she? Certainly she had long ago forgotten the stranger who had saved her son. Most likely she had taken another husband and given away the kingdom of her love, just like the poor woman in the stable must have offered her heart to every other man who would spare her a couple of coins, no matter her promise to him.

There were so many thoughts and so many days and nights to think them. Their weight over time caved in the strong chest of the rower. His breath became labored. His temples went gray first, then his whole head. His eyes sank even further into their sockets, while his skin gradually turned to leather.

WHEN THE LITTLE CZAR was finally released from his service, they
had to carry him to land. He wasn't
useful on the galley anymore; he was good for
nothing but death. The port where which they
landed was the same one in which thirty years
earlier he had let himself be put into shackles.

For a few hours he lay against a curbstone in the
shadows, letting the wind blow around him. After
thirty years of must and stuffy heat belowdecks,
he immensely enjoyed the air caressing his skin.
Face to face with the gleaming silver mirror of the
water, he closed his eyes. He had gotten to know

the murderous cruelty of the sea, and its smile could no longer seduce him. Packs of dogs from the harbor sniffed at him, lifting their legs on his shoulder. He didn't chase them away. He had yet to reawaken to life. Occasionally he nodded off for a while, doubting that he would ever be able to leave the port on his own. His legs wouldn't be carrying him any time soon; he had scarcely used them for years. But he would be content if let alone in this place so that he could fall asleep forever.

Toward evening, however, a man came by. He looked well off, and his retinue of servants suggested that he was a distinguished personage. He stopped in front of the little czar, looked at him for a long while, and asked where he came from.

The fourth king merely raised his hand and pointed out to the sea. From there he had come, he said, and he didn't want to talk.

Had he been released from a galley? asked the man, observing with a shudder the leathery skin of

57

his naked ankles, which had been clasped in irons for thirty years.

The little czar nodded. "Yes, today," was all that he was able to say.

"Can you walk by yourself?" the man asked. The little czar shook his head with a timid smile. That meant no.

"Get a stretcher," the stranger commanded two of his servants. They went off, leaving a third one behind. The rich man continued to speak: "Starting today you will stay at my house until you've been nursed back to health."

The little czar couldn't believe his ears. He wanted to thank the stranger, but before he could get a word past his lips the man said: "Don't thank me! And the woman whom you might thank is no longer alive. She was my mother. Till the day of her death she obliged me to take in all slaves freed from the galleys and to have them cared for in my house until they recovered their strength.

I've never liked fulfilling that last wish of hers," he said harshly, "and that is not likely to change, for almost all they throw off the ships are scofflaws better suited to enter jail than my elegant house. But...my mother said that she once saw a good man walk into a galley, and for his sake she extracted from me the promise I'm carrying out. If you are different from the ones before you, that will honor her memory, and the whim of her soft woman's heart will seem a little less foolish to me."

The little czar lay against the curbstone and looked the rich man in the eye. For a long time he said nothing, overwhelmed by his memories. He searched the face of the man before him. Could he make out the features of a helpless boy who had been shuffled to the galley like a lamb to slaughter thirty years ago? Then he said, almost in a whisper: "Well, well, so it was your mother, my lord? I..." But he broke off, not wanting to give himself away. "I have always known, for thirty years I knew," he had begun to say. "I won't cause your good mother any disgrace," he finally said. "You are surely the oldest of her sons?"

The stranger nodded. "Yes," he said. "It isn't always easy to be the oldest son; it entails numerous and awkward duties."

The little czar would have been tempted to reply, but luckily the two servants arrived just then with a stretcher, taking away his chance to speak. Uttering a deep groan, he let them lift him onto the stretcher.

From that day on the little czar lived in a distant room in the house of the rich merchant, who never tired of complaining to the world how much he disliked the service his mother had forced him to accept. Not a single one of these men, he felt, was worth his mother's compassion. Moreover, he thought that all of them should be carried from the galleys to jail, and from there straight to the slaughterhouse. He was a tough master, the

rich merchant. He had worked his way up with great toil from modest beginnings and a childhood distressed by the debts of his father, who had died young. Now his wealth and success silenced anyone who would have dared to remind him that his own father had met his end on a galley. But still the promise he had given his mother was kept.

The servants shared all this with the little czar, who lived quietly in his remote room like a shadow, regaining his strength. Most of his time was spent recalling the past, and since the woman for whom he had entered the galley was dead, he had only the star to think about, and he wondered whatever had become of the king of all times and places.

"You are the exception to the rule," said the rich merchant with reluctant respect when the little czar came to take leave and give thanks. "Unless it turns out that you just went about being a villain more skillfully than the others," he added, full of distrust. "But I hope I am right for the first time. I would prefer that for the sake of my mother."

"So would I," the little czar agreed, "blessed be her memory."

The merchant looked at him, somewhat discon-certed. He hadn't expected such words, but the little czar had already turned away and gone. He didn't want his tears to be seen.

ONCE MORE HE SET OUT on the roads that had been his home for so long before the bench in the galley took their place. He still remembered where his star had shone for the last time and plunged its long, golden tail to the earth. As if out of old habit he went off in this direction, and it seemed that he had made the right choice, for the streets were filled with people. Had tramps become so much more numerous, or did the south hold special enticements? He surveyed the travelers and soon found that they weren't tramps at all. On the contrary, they were upright citizens. Entire families, more or less elegant, were streaming on this fine spring day down to the south, where they had planned to attend a festival in the great city. Of course, the mass of people swept along with it some of the brotherhood that always show up in times of idleness and festivity: beggars, jugglers, and peddlers.

The little czar passed by someone who could only drag himself with groans on his way to the big fair that might well bring in alms enough to hold his soul and body together for the short time he would still live. Another time a sturdier group of wanderers overtook him. They looked down on him with the malicious pleasure of being stronger competitors in the race to milk people's compassion.

One of these figures, an old woman, stayed in his field of vision for days. She carried no goods, which led him to believe that she was out not to peddle but to beg. However, she walked rather robustly, using a walking stick. She went at about the same pace as the little czar; otherwise he couldn't have kept her in his sight for so long. She seemed to rest when he did, spend the night where he did, and set off in the morning at the same time as he. She appeared to have the same energy, similar habits, and perhaps the same sort of fatigue.

When on the third day he saw her exactly as far in front of him as before, it struck him as odd, as if his own shadow was preceding him by just that much. She aroused his curiosity and got him thinking. Should he try to catch up with her, or would she speed up her steps if he did? Then again, he was tired and should let this whole puzzle rest. "Perhaps," he thought, "this is just my imagination. Most things that keep us busy in life are just disguises worn by fate, and love is no more than that. But love is surely the fairest disguise of all — for the cruelest lesson."

By the following day the great city must have

been close. Throngs of people from eastern and western roads pushed onto the route to the south As the crowd kept growing, the little czar became terribly lonely. And he had now lost sight of the beggar woman whose face he had actually never seen. But she was the last thing that had at least briefly become familiar, only to disappear again. It was as if his own shadow had been taken away. Now, he thought, he should rest and reflect on what he was here for.

Later that afternoon the domes of a gigantic temple glistened from afar in the city built on four hills. At the sight of it the travelers cried out in ecstasy and praise, and they rushed ahead in order to arrive within its walls before evening. Only the little czar slackened his pace. He had no desire to bed down in the city that night. Would he ever want to?

Around sunset he saw a small grove of olive trees on a hill just in front of the city gates. He left the main road and climbed panting up a narrow path. He hoped he could spend the night under the trees or in a gardener's hut.

The place appeared homey and at the same time depressing. The gardens seemed to belong to rich people. None of the thick, shady enclosures lacked careful tending, but there wasn't a living soul to be seen. Just once the little czar thought he saw a shadow vanish among the shrubbery. But when not a twig moved and no sound could be heard, he dismissed it as a trick of his imagination in a lonesome place. Or maybe the shadow had been some vagrant, no more interested in meeting people than he was.

WHEN HE FOUND A WELL, no doubt used by a gardener during the day, the little czar took a long and generous drink to quench his thirst. Then he looked around and listened. In the distance the blast of mighty trumpets resounded, borne by the calm evening air. Under the trees, where the earth was damp around the well, the tiny hum of a swarm of gnats rose and sank. Crickets sang in the bushes. For a long time the little czar stood motionless, as if pondering whether he had to move on. Then, giving in to his fatigue, he walked up a narrow path along a broad arch of rocks. The night was coming on quickly, and he wished to spend it under the shelter of the rocks.

But the deep recess into which he headed was ... already occupied. The little czar was startled. An old woman sat there, looking as if she had been there since time immemorial. She sat as motionless as if carved in stone. He backed away, but she had already seen him. Now it struck him as ridiculous that he had even thought of retreating; surely this woman was no more an invited guest than he. She was an old beggar, worn by wind and weather. She too had probably shied away from entering the bursting city that evening and decided to spend the night here.

Without paying her much heed, he made himself at home as he usually did. He sought out a flat rock to lean against and placed his right hand on the back of his neck as a pillow. Then he looked up at the stars. The old woman, who nodded off into long periods of silence, seemed inclined to chat

when awake. She began to query him, as beggars
often do. Where were his best places? How did he
set about making a big haul? Had he ever feigned
diseases to win pity, and if so which ones worked
best? Where in his estimation were the authorities
most dangerous and the people most softhearted?

To most of these questions the little czar could
think of no answer. He didn't have the sort of ex-
perience the old woman did. And it wasn't long
before he fell asleep. When, shortly after, the
woman's voice woke him up again, at first he
felt angry. She wanted to know where he had
come from.

The little czar listened to her question. The recess where they sat made their voices sound three
times stronger than usual.

"From where?" he asked still drugged with sleep.
"Ah, from far away..." Then he named the city
where they had carried him off the galley and where
the merchant had taken him in.

The old woman kept silent, and in the night's darkness he could no longer see her.

She jokingly asked if he was part of the brotherhood.

"What brotherhood?" the little czar wanted to know.

"Well, the one that gives people an opportunity to do good as the law commands."

This struck him as a strangely elevated explanation for begging. "No," he said quietly after a while. "I am not of that brotherhood. But wait! Strictly speaking, yes, only..." Most of the time no one had taken advantage of the opportunity to help him. But maybe that was how life was for most people.

The old woman giggled in the dark. "One has to give them something, too," she said, in her aged and cracked voice.

"As a beggar? Give something to the people?" the little czar asked in surprise.

"Oh, yes," the old woman said, "nobody is so poor that he doesn't have anything to give. And if only people would feel that, they would do good. That's how people are. Only the Almighty gives to empty hands."

The little czar was now completely awake. "What can a panhandler," he asked, "give in return to his benefactor?"

"Ah," replied the old woman serenely, "all that he has."

"Then why is he begging to begin with, if he already has something?" the little czar asked impatiently. "The fact that he is begging proves he has nothing!"

From the old woman's corner came silence, and the little czar thought he had carried his point against the childish woman.

But then she said, "Ah, you seem no younger than I am, yet you don't have a clue. Obviously, a beggar cannot give back the same, but something else, which the giver might need more than money. A look, perhaps, a word — something that lights up the heart and spirit of the other, that builds a little more self-esteem or eases his guilty conscience. There is so much…"

"Much!" the little czar repeated, shaking his head and secretly smiling.

"I" — the woman's voice sounded in the dark — "once gave away all I had, and…yes, I was still young then!"

The little czar thought the old woman meant to say that at some point in her youth she had sold her body for a handout. But he didn't want to ask further, since the woman had fallen silent again.

"I know what you're thinking," she said a little while later, in her bodiless yet resonant voice. "You think I sold my body for money. No, no! I have had men, and I have had children, but not for money or to do someone a favor. That is not what I'm talking about. Folly is folly, and sin is sin. And love is an excuse for both. No, I have given away much more, but you can believe me that to this day I have been receiving in return."

"What did you give?" the little czar asked, "and how do you still receive in return?"

A long silence covered the distance between them. Curious, the little czar gazed at the spot where the woman was sitting.

"It was about thirty years ago. I gave away my heart," said the woman, with more depth in her voice than before. "To a man who treated me well, and with compassion. He was a very good man. I was at the time young and beautiful, and in desperate need. I did tell him then that my heart was his kingdom, but I don't know whether he believed me. Who would believe a poor young woman anyway? No, I didn't even know whether he accepted my gift. But I gave it to him as he rode on and have never since taken it back. Neither by accident nor deliberately. But ever since...ever since I have felt this happiness that a very good and compassionate man owns my heart. For thirty years now I have taken delight in it, and day by day my faithfulness keeps completing the gift. See ... nothing gets lost," the woman whispered, and the little czar heard her yawn.

"No," he agreed, "you are right about that. Nothing gets lost! But no one knows where it hides, or if it ever comes back, or when."

He was glad that she kept silent, letting this remark pass. The lucid tranquillity of the night allowed his thoughts to wander thirty years back into the little barn where he had first found her. She had just given birth to a baby girl, and he had cut diapers from a roll of the finest linen. Thirty years ago! Now she was an old woman, and he was an old man. Each had gone off on distant journeys, but both had finally found the same road to the same place — one not knowing of the other.

Now he knew that it was she he had mistaken for his own shadow for days, and that all he seemed to have lost he had, in fact, gained. Moreover, for thirty years he had already owned what he never truly believed in: the kingdom of a heart promised to him in the dark of a stable. So, he was still a king! No matter how unworthy he felt, or that he had lost his only chance to serve the supreme ruler of all times and places.

With tears in his eyes, he looked up at the stars. His heart was with the worn woman. He was certain that she had not recognized him any more than he would have recognized her without hearing her story. Day by day she had taken delight in being faithful to him, he recalled her telling. Wasn't he, then, unimaginably rich, even without a crown or a country? His thoughts got lost among the milky veils of the sky, and he may have fallen asleep for a while. Then raucous noises invaded the alcove. The old woman, he sensed, was disturbed by them, too. Their recess echoed the approaching voices like a seashell. "Ay! These big cities," he heard the woman mutter. "Always this shouting! Now they go crazy even at night!"

The little czar sat tensely, ready to hurry off through the bushes. Voices rumbled and arms rattled, though it seemed that they were not out to search the garden. What did the whole thing mean? Perhaps the night watch was out looking for someone. The little czar was glad that they hadn't come closer. Peace seemed to return, and once again they could hear the foliage whisper in the wind, drops of dew dripping from wherever they had formed, and the pulse of faint sounds that make the night still deeper. The little czar fell asleep again.

When he woke up at dawn, he found himself alone. He hadn't heard the old woman leave. He had been sound asleep, just like in his youth when he dreamt of kvass and lightly salted cucumbers. Or perhaps he had mistaken her steps for one of the sounds of the night. But she was gone. He missed her company. Surely, he would not see her again. There were too many beggars sitting along the streets of this city to make it worthwhile to search for just one. And why should he see her again? He already knew her story, and even today he would receive the gift of faithfulness from her delighted heart.

His own ailing heart sensed that the day would be hot and muggy. The warm, wet air beneath the foliage was already weighing heavily on his weakened chest. He labored to breathe. Beyond the garden, haze drifted over the city, making the silhouettes of its roofs and domes quiver. The little czar grew dizzy as his gaze found nowhere to rest. He didn't want to leave and decided to stay for a while longer.

Noon was approaching when he finally walked down the hill to the main road that he had taken the day before. It led to the city gates. The crush of people would be worse today, for at sunset the festival began and the faithful had to retreat and be still. The last, late-arriving caravans, hurried along by their whip-wielding drivers, rolled toward the gates. Bleating sheep to be sacrificed at the temple were so tightly packed together that they looked like a drifting carpet of fluffy white wool. And where the road left no room for another beast, a man would make his way. When the little czar joined the masses, he was at once squeezed in, ground like grain, and sucked behind the walls, unable to command his own direction.

Caught beneath the huge blocks of the gate, he might have collapsed and would surely have been trampled to death by the mob coming after him, but at the last minute he seized hold of a donkey's tail and let himself be pulled out by the ass. For a moment he remembered his dead friend Vanyka, the pony that had carried him so securely. But once inside the gates he could no longer dwell on the past. His old, weary head could hardly grasp the present.

His eyes opened wide to take hold of all the strange things around him. His ears could make out a sound in this sea of noise only when it was constantly repeated. The throng seemed to shout for a king. The little czar did not understand who he was or whether the crowd was out to adore him or to revolt.

For a while he let himself be carried along by the flow of people — a river swollen into a torrent. With everyone else he hurried toward the city's center. But his strength was failing, and he maneuvered himself into a protective gateway. He leaned on the walls of the alcove and closed his eyes. Never had he felt so weak. The noise of the pushing crowds jumbled in the background. He didn't want to see the hordes of people, who seemed to grow increasingly malicious. "Probably," he thought, "this is an uprising. Although in a crowd joy and anger often look similar in scary ways . . ."

But what kind of a king was this?

His breath stopped short, and he feared his heart would stop beating. Suddenly a thought invaded his mind and dizziness overtook his senses. "They have the greatest one of all, and they want to make him the least." He heard a familiar voice rise from the crowd, but in his confusion he couldn't make out where it came from. Then in the shadow of the gateway he saw the old woman from the garden.

He stared at her. Then he stuttered repeatedly before he managed to speak: "What are you saying? Who are you talking about?"

She looked at him with what he thought was a mocking smile. "You have wandered around all these roads in Samaria and Galilee and don't even know this?"

He shook his head in silence.

His heart pounded as if it were about to burst. "They have a king, whom Holy Scriptures say is the son of God himself. He has healed the sick and raised the dead. But now the people want to crucify him."

"How...how do you know?" the little czar asked. Already he was about to step out from the gateway.

The old woman looked at him with gentle disdain. "One doesn't get only alms," she said "One also gets information."

The little czar was beside himself. A king whom Holy Scriptures say is the son of God, and he... "Tell me, how old is this king?" he demanded.

"Him?" she responded calmly. "They say he is around thirty."

"Thirty? Thirty, you say?" the little czar asked, gasping for breath.

The old woman nodded. As he stared at her in

bewilderment, it seemed to him as if her head was the pendulum of a clock winding down, moving back and forth more and more slowly. But he didn't know if it was she who was going crazy or he himself.

"Thirty, thirty," he murmured, as if that were the world's greatest puzzle — and the deepest mystery of his own life. "Thirty," he said a little bit louder, raising his head. He looked at the old woman. "Wasn't that..." — then he completed the sentence, totally forgetting himself — "...when you had your child in the barn, and I wrapped your baby in linen?"

Now the old woman stared at him, her eyes wide open and her mouth showing no teeth. Her claw-like hands trembled. She said nothing, but it was clear that now she knew who he was.

"I take your heart with me, your whole heart, and forever!" the little czar stammered. Then he rushed off into a crowd of latecomers pushing toward the center of the city. One single time he looked back. The old woman sat motionless in the gateway, her meager body crouched against the walls as if cut in stone.

He didn't see her fall; he had already turned.

UP THE ALLEY, across the streets and squares...wherever he went, it was too late. He could still sense the great excitement, but whatever had happened was past. Where to? The little czar didn't know the city. The never-ending crowds confused his sense of direction.

"The king...? Which way? Where?" he finally asked a man passing by. What he wanted to know was where they had taken the king. The stranger was puzzled by the little czar's confusion and pointed him in a direction that many people were heading. That path led away from the city, and while he was walking the little czar sensed strongly that he was getting closer to where he wanted to be. People stood alongside the road, left there after what had happened, like the surf leaves a spray of foam on the beach.

The little czar barely raised his head. He no longer needed directions from others; he just needed to hurry. He passed women in tears, angry men, slackers and bystanders, but nothing could distract him anymore. "The king...! The supreme ruler! Holy Scriptures and prophets announced him," he thought. "And now his own people have revolted against him." He was the same king whose arrival on earth the star had announced and for whom he, the little czar, had left his beloved Russia. And the three elegant magi had traveled from afar to find him. How could that be? How could that ever happen?

This did not make sense. As the little czar walked on, houses gave way to open fields, gently rising up a hill. Hardly anyone had made it to this site; they had preferred to stay down below and gawk at the scene from a safe distance. On the top of the hill, slaves had mounted three crosses, and three people had been nailed to the wood. Up there, and nowhere else in the world, was his king!

For a moment it looked as if the little czar hesitated to go forward. In reality, though, his weakness and a sudden knowledge of reality had overwhelmed him. He stopped short, he swayed, but then he continued to climb the slope, his back bent and his breathing irregular. How his feet kept on carrying him, he didn't know. These...surely, these were his last steps. The first he had made thirty years before. And all the steps in between he had made toward the same destination. Had he come too late? Had he once again come too late?

The fourth king, the little czar of Russia, raised his head as he walked. He looked to the three crosses, especially to the man in the middle. Skeletons bleached by the sun and moldering bones got in the way of his feet. Sweat streamed down his body. Nothing, it seemed, could divert his attention. But suddenly he stopped and clutched at his heart pierced by pain. His face was gray, and his lips turned a dark blue, like the color of the berries he had so often picked for a free lunch.

He continued to walk, though more slowly with every step. He now held his head back so that he would not lose sight of the cross. And the more he had to pause and rest, the more clearly and intimately he saw his supreme ruler, his king of all times and places. For him he had left his homeland thirty years ago, while still a young man. The little czar knew that he was the man on the cross. But how he knew, he had already forgotten. It had happened when the man on the cross looked him in the eye, just once. That was when he knew forever.

He looked at him, and he was looked at by him. The little czar felt complete peace and purpose and

joy. Then his heart failed, just stopped beating, and he collapsed.

"I have nothing," thought the little czar, and he was deeply ashamed. "I have nothing left of all the things that I wanted to bring you. The gold, the precious stones, the linen and furs, not even the sweet linden honey that my mother prepared. All of it squandered, everything gone. Forgive me!... But Russia..." Then the light started fading before his eyes.

But suddenly he was reminded of the poor woman's heart, which she had given him for a kingdom. He thought about his own heart, too. It was the only thing still his to give. As he lay on the ground in the midst of rotting bones, his face rested on a pillow of wild thyme. His body was wrapped in its perfume. Barely conscious, the little czar whispered: "But my heart, Lord. My heart... and her heart.... Our hearts, will you take them?"